# THE MAN WHO SAVED THE EARTH

**Austin Hall** (1885–1933) was an American writer, novelist and journalist. He wrote several science fiction stories and short fantasy tales for pulp magazines. *The Man Who Saved the Earth* (1919), *Into the Infinite* (1919) and *Almost Immortal* (1916) are a few of his well-known works.

# THE MAN WHO SAVED THE EARTH

# Austin Hall

RUPA

Published by
Rupa Publications India Pvt. Ltd 2023
7/16, Ansari Road, Daryaganj
New Delhi 110002

*Sales Centres:*

Prayagraj Bengaluru Chennai
Hyderabad Jaipur Kathmandu
Kolkata Mumbai

Edition copyright © Rupa Publications India Pvt. Ltd 2023

All rights reserved.
No part of this publication may be reproduced, transmitted, or stored in a retrieval system, in any form or by any means, electronic, mechanical, photocopying, recording or otherwise, without the prior permission of the publisher.

P-ISBN: 978-93-5702-225-5
E-ISBN: 978-93-5702-227-9

First impression 2023

10 9 8 7 6 5 4 3 2 1

Printed in India

This book is sold subject to the condition that it shall not,
by way of trade or otherwise, be lent, resold, hired out, or otherwise circulated, without the publisher's prior consent, in any form of binding or cover other than that in which it is published.

# CONTENTS

*Prologue* — 7

1. The Beginning — 9
2. The Poison Pall — 15
3. The Mountain That Was — 24
4. "Man—A Great Little Bug" — 32
5. Approaching Disaster — 38
6. A Race to Save the World — 44
7. A Riven Continent — 51
8. The Man Who Saved the Earth — 57
9. The Most Terrific Moment in History — 64

# PROLOGUE

*Not a sound; the whole works a complicated mass covering a hundred acres, driving with a silence that was magic. Not a whir nor friction. Like a living composite body pulsing and breathing the strange and mysterious force that had been evolved from Huyck's*

*theory of kinetics. The four great steel conduits running from the globes down the side of the mountain. In the center at a point midway between the globes, a massive steel needle hung on a pivot and pointed directly at the sun.*

We read of the days when the powers of radium were yet unknown. It is told us that burns were produced by incautiously carrying a tube of radium salts in the pocket. And here in this story we are told of a different power, opalescence, due to another element. It can destroy mountains, excavate cavities of immeasurable depths and kill human beings and animals in multitude. The story opens with a poor little boy experimenting with a burning glass. Then he becomes the hero of the story—he studies and eventually finds himself able to destroy the earth. He exceeds Archimedes in his power. And he suddenly finds that he has unlocked a power that threatens this very destruction. And the story depicts his horror at the Frankenstein which he had unloosed, and tells of his wild efforts to save humanity, and of the loss of the cosmic discoveries of the little newsboy grown up to be a great scientist.

# 1

# THE BEGINNING

Even the beginning. From the start the whole thing has the precision of machine work. Fate and its working—and the wonderful Providence which watches over Man and his future. The whole thing unerring: the incident, the work, the calamity, and the martyr. In the retrospect of disaster we may all of us grow strong in wisdom. Let us go into history.

A hot July day. A sun of scant pity, and a staggering street; panting thousands dragging along, hatless; fans and parasols; the sultry vengeance of a real day of summer. A day of bursting tires; hot pavements, and wrecked endeavor, heartaches for the seashore, for leafy bowers beside rippling water, a day of broken hopes and listless ambition.

Perhaps Fate chose the day because of its heat and because of its natural benefit on fecundity. We have no way of knowing. But we do know this: the date, the time, the meeting; the boy with the burning glass and the old doctor. So commonplace, so trivial and hidden in obscurity! Who would have guessed it? Yet it is—after the creation—one of the most important dates in the world's history.

This is saying a whole lot. Let us go into it and see what it amounts to. Let us trace the thing out in history, weigh it up and balance it with sequence.

Of Charley Huyck we know nothing up to this day. It is a thing which, for some reason, he has always kept hidden. Recent investigation as to his previous life and antecedents have availed us nothing. Perhaps he could have told us; but as he has gone down as the world's great martyr, there is no hope of gaining from his lips what we would so like to know.

After all, it does not matter. We have the day—the incident, and its purport, and its climax of sequence to the day of the great disaster. Also we have the blasted mountains and the lake of blue water which will ever live with his memory. His greatness is not of warfare, nor personal ambition; but of all mankind. The wreaths that we bestow upon him have no doubtful color. The man who saved the earth!

From such a beginning, Charley Huyck, lean and frail of body, with, even then, the wistfulness of the idealist, and the eyes of a poet. Charley Huyck, the boy, crossing the hot pavement with his pack of papers; the much treasured piece of glass in his pocket, and the sun which only he should master burning down upon him. A moment out of the ages; the turning of a straw destined to out-balance all the previous accumulation of man's history.

The sun was hot and burning, and the child—he could not have been more than ten—cast a glance over his shoulder. It was in the way of calculation. In the heyday of childhood he was not dragged down by the heat and weather: he had the enthusiasm of his half-score of years and the joy of the plaything. We will not presume to call it the spirit of the scientist, though it was, perhaps, the spark of latent investigation that was destined to lead so far.

A moment picked out of destiny! A boy and a plaything. Uncounted millions of boys have played with glass and the sun rays. Who cannot remember the little, round-burning dot in the palm of the hand and the subsequent exclamation? Charley Huyck had found a new toy, it was a simple thing and as old as glass. Fate will ever be so in her working.

And the doctor? Why should he have been waiting? If it was not destiny, it was at least an accumulation of moment. In the heavy eye-glasses, the square, close-cut beard; and his uncompromising fact-seeking expression. Those who knew Dr. Robold are strong in the affirmation that he was the antithesis of all emotion. He was the sternest product of science: unbending, hardened by experiment, and caustic in his condemnation of the frailness of human nature.

It had been his one function to topple over the castles of the foolish; with his hard-seeing wisdom he had spotted sophistry where we thought it not. Even into the castles of science he had gone like a juggernaut. It is hard to have one's theories derided—yea, even for a scientist—and to be called a fool! Dr. Robold knew no middle language; he was not relished by science.

His memory, as we have it, is that of an eccentric. A man of slight compassion, abrupt of manner and with no tact in speaking. Genius is often so; it is a strange fact that many of the greatest of men have been denied by their fellows. A great man and laughter. He was not accepted.

None of us know to-day what it cost Dr. Robold. He was not the man to tell us. Perhaps Charley Huyck might; but his lips are sealed forever. We only know that he retired to the mountain, and of the subsequent flood of benefits that rained upon mankind. And we still denied him. The great cynic on the mountain. Of the secrets of the place we know little. He was not the man to accept the investigator; he despised the curious. He had been laughed at—let be—he would work alone on the great moment of the future.

In the light of the past we may well bend knee to the doctor and his protégé, Charley Huyck. Two men and destiny! What would we be without them? One shudders to think.

A little thing, and yet one of the greatest moments in the world's history. It must have been Fate. Why was it that this stern man, who hated all emotion, should so have unbended at this moment? That we cannot answer. But we can conjecture. Mayhap it is this: We were all wrong; we accepted the man's exterior and profession as the fact of his marrow.

No man can lose all emotion. The doctor, was, after all, even as ourselves—he was human. Whatever may be said, we have the certainty of that moment—and of Charley Huyck.

The sun's rays were hot; they were burning; the pavements were intolerable; the baked air in the canyoned street was dancing like that of an oven; a day of dog-days. The boy crossing the street; his arms full of papers, and the glass bulging in his little hip-pocket.

At the curb he stopped. With such a sun it was impossible to long forget his plaything. He drew it carefully out of his pocket, lay down a paper and began distancing his glass for the focus. He did not notice the man beside him. Why should he? The round dot, the brownish smoke, the red spark and the flash of flame! He stamped upon it. A moment out of boyhood; an experimental miracle as old as the age of glass, and just as delightful. The boy had spoiled the name of a great Governor of a great State; but the paper was still salable. He had had his moment. Mark that moment.

A hand touched his shoulder. The lad leaped up. "Yessir. *Star* or *Bulletin*?"

"I'll take one of each," said the man. "There now. I was just watching you. Do you know what you were doing?"

"Yessir. Burning paper. Startin' fire. That's the way the Indians did it."

The man smiled at the perversion of fact. There is not such a distance between sticks and glass in the age of childhood.

"I know," he said—"the Indians. But do you know how it was done; the why—why the paper began to blaze?"

"Yessir."

"All right, explain."

The boy looked up at him. He was a city boy and used to the streets. Here was some old high-brow challenging his wisdom. Of course he knew. "It's the sun."

"There," laughed the man. "Of course. You said you knew, but you don't. Why doesn't the sun, without the glass, burn the paper? Tell me that."

The boy was still looking up at him; he saw that the man was not like the others on the street. It may be that the strange intimacy kindled into being at that moment. Certainly it was a strange unbending for the doctor.

"It would if it was hot enough or you could get enough of it together."

"Ah! Then that is what the glass is for, is it?"

"Yessir."

"Concentration?"

"Con— I don't know, sir. But it's the sun. She's sure some hot. I know a lot about the sun, sir. I've studied it with the glass. The glass picks up all the rays and puts them in one hole and that's what burns the paper.

"It's lots of fun. I'd like to have a bigger one; but it's all I've got. Why, do you know, if I had a glass big enough and a place to stand, I'd burn up the earth?"

The old man laughed. "Why, Archimedes! I thought you were dead."

"My name ain't Archimedes. It's Charley Huyck."

Again the old man laughed.

"Oh, is it? Well, that's a good name, too. And if you keep on you'll make it famous as the name of the other." Wherein he was foretelling history. "Where do you live?"

The boy was still looking. Ordinarily he would not have told, but he motioned back with his thumb.

"I don't live; I room over on Brennan Street."

"Oh, I see. You room. Where's your mother?"

"Search me; I never saw her."

"I see; and your father?"

"How do I know. He went floating when I was four years old."

"Floating?"

"Yessir—to sea."

"So your mother's gone and your father's floating. Archimedes is adrift. You go to school?"

"Yessir"

"What reader?"

"No reader. Sixth grade."

"I see. What school?"

"School Twenty-six. Say, it's hot. I can't stand here all day. I've got to sell my papers."

The man pulled out a purse.

"I'll take the lot," he said. Then kindly: "My boy, I would like to have you go with me."

It was a strange moment. A little thing with the fates looking on. When destiny plays she picks strange moments. This was one. Charley Huyck went with Dr. Robold.

# 2

## THE POISON PALL

We all of us remember that fatal day when the news startled all of Oakland. No one can forget it. At first it read like a newspaper hoax, in spite of the oft-proclaimed veracity of the press, and we were inclined to laughter. 'Twixt wonder at the story and its impossibilities we were not a little enthused at the nerve of the man who put it over.

It was in the days of dry reading. The world had grown populous and of well-fed content. Our soap-box artists had come to the point at last where they preached, not disaster, but a full-bellied thanks for the millennium that was here. A period of Utopian quietness—no villain around the corner; no man to covet the ox of his neighbor.

Quiet reading, you'll admit. Those were the days of the millennium. Nothing ever happened. Here's hoping they never come again. And then:

Honestly, we were not to blame for bestowing blessing out of our hearts upon that newspaperman. Even if it were a hoax, it was at least something.

At high noon. The clock in the city hall had just struck the hour that held the post 'twixt a.m. and p.m., a hot day with a sky that was clear and azure; a quiet day of serene peace and contentment. A strange and a portent moment. Looking back and over the miracle we may conjecture that it was the clearness of the atmosphere and the brightness of the sun that helped to the impact of the disaster. Knowing what we know now we can appreciate the impulse of natural phenomena. It was *not* a miracle.

The spot: Fourteenth and Broadway, Oakland, California.

Fortunately the thousands of employees in the stores about had not yet come out for their luncheons. The lapse that it takes to put a hat on, or to pat a ribbon, saved a thousand lives. One shudders to think of what would have happened had the spot been crowded. Even so, it was too impossible and too terrible to be true. Such things could not happen.

At high noon: Two street-cars crossing Fourteenth on Broadway—two cars with the same joggle and bump and the same aspect of any of a hundred thousand at a traffic corner. The wonder is—there were so few people. A Telegraph car outgoing, and a Broadway car coming in. The traffic policeman at his post had just given his signal. Two automobiles were passing and a single pedestrian, so it is said, was working his way diagonally across the corner. Of this we are not certain.

It was a moment that impinged on miracle. Even as we recount it, knowing, as we do, the explanation, we sense the impossibility of the event. A phenomenon that holds out and, in spite of our findings, lingers into the miraculous. To be and not to be. One moment life and action, an ordinary scene of existent monotony; and the next moment nothing. The spot, the intersection of the street, the passing street-cars, the two automobiles, pedestrian, the policeman—non-existent! When events are instantaneous reports are apt to be misleading. This is what we find.

Some of those who beheld it, report a flash of bluish white light; others that it was of a greenish or even a violet hue; and others, no doubt of stronger vision, that it was not only of a predominant color but that it was shot and sparkled with a myriad specks of flame and burning.

It gave no warning and it made no sound; not even a whir. Like a hot breath out of the void. Whatever the forces that had focused, they were destruction. There was no Fourteenth and Broadway. The two automobiles, the two street-cars, the pedestrian, the policeman had been whiffed away as if they had never existed. In place of the intersection of the thoroughfares was a yawning gulf that looked down into the center of the earth to a depth of nausea.

It was instantaneous; it was without sound; no warning. A tremendous force of unlimited potentiality had been loosed to kinetic violence. It was the suddenness and the silence that belied credence. We were accustomed to associate all disaster with confusion; calamity has an affinity with pandemonium, all things of terror climax into sound. In this case there was no sound. Hence the wonder.

A hole or bore forty feet in diameter. Without a particle of warning and without a bit of confusion. The spectators one and all aver that at first they took it for nothing more than the effect of startled eyesight. Almost subtle. It was not until after a full minute's reflection that they became aware that a miracle had been wrought before their faces. Then the crowd rushed up and with awe and now awakened terror gazed down into that terrible pit.

We say "Terrible" because in this case it is an exact adjective.

The strangest hole that man ever looked into. It was so deep that at first it appeared to have no bottom; not even the strongest eyesight could penetrate the smoldering blackness that shrouded the depths descending. It took a stout heart and courage to stand and hold one's head on the brink for even a minute.

It was straight and precipitous; a perfect circle in shape; with sides as smooth as the effect of machine work, the pavement and stone curb had been cut as if by a razor. Of the two street-cars, two automobiles and their occupants there was nothing. The whole thing so silent and complete. Not even the spectators could really believe it.

It was a hard thing to believe. The newspapers themselves, when the news came clamoring, accepted it with reluctance. It was too much like a hoax. Not until the most trusted reporters had gone and had wired in their reports would they even consider it. Then the whole world sat up and took notice.

A miracle! Like Oakland's Press we all of us doubted that hole. We had attained almost everything that was worth the knowing; we were the masters of the earth and its secrets and we were proud of our wisdom, naturally we refused such reports all out of reason. It must be a hoax.

But the wires were persistent. Came corroboration. A reliable news-gathering organization soon was coming through with elaborate and detailed accounts of just what was happening. We had the news from the highest and most reputable authority.

And still we doubted. It was the story itself that brought the doubting; its touch on miracle. It was too easy to pick on the reporter. There might be a hole, and all that; but this thing of no explanation! A bomb perhaps? No noise? Some new explosive? No such thing? Well, how did we know? It was better than a miracle.

Then came the scientists. As soon as could be men of great

minds had been hustled to the scene. The world had long been accustomed to accept without quibble the dictum of these great specialists of fact. With their train of accomplishments behind them we would hardly be consistent were we to doubt them.

We know the scientist and his habits. He is the one man who will believe nothing until it is proved. It is his profession, and for that we pay him. He can catch the smallest bug that ever crawled out of an atom and give it a name so long that a Polish wrestler, if he had to bear it, would break under the burden. It is his very knack of getting in under that has given us our civilization. You don't baffle a scientist in our Utopia. It can't be done. Which is one of the very reasons why we began to believe in the miracle.

In a few moments a crowd of many thousands had gathered about the spot; the throng grew so dense that there was peril of some of them being crowded into the pit at the center. It took all the spare policemen of the city to beat them back far enough to string ropes from the corners. For blocks the streets were packed with wondering thousands. Street traffic was impossible. It was necessary to divert the cars to a roundabout route to keep the arteries open to the suburbs.

Wild rumors spread over the city. No one knew how many passengers had been upon the street-cars. The officials of the company, from the schedule, could pick the numbers of the cars and their crews; but who could tell of the occupants?

Telephones rang with tearful pleadings. When the first rumors of the horror leaked out every wife and mother felt the clutch of panic at her heartstrings. It was a moment of historical psychology. Out of our books we had read of this strange phase of human nature that was wont to rise like a mad screeching thing out of disaster. We had never had it in Utopia.

It was rumbling at first and out of exaggeration; as the tale passed farther back to the waiting thousands it gained with the repetition. Grim and terrible enough in fact, it ratioed up with reiteration. Perhaps after all it was not psychology. The average impulse of the human mind does not even up so exactly. In the light of what we now know it may have been the poison that had leaked into the air; the new element that was permeating the atmosphere of the city.

At first it was spasmodic. The nearest witnesses of the disaster were the first victims. A strange malady began to spot out among those of the crowd who had been at the spot of contact. This is to be noticed. A strange affliction which from the virulence and rapidity of action was quite puzzling to the doctors.

Those among the physicians who would consent to statement gave it out that it was breaking down of tissue. Which of course it was; the new element that was radiating through the atmosphere of the city. They did not know it then.

The pity of it! The subtle, odorless pall was silently shrouding out over the city. In a short time the hospitals were full and it was necessary to call in medical aid from San Francisco. They had not even time for diagnosis. The new plague was fatal almost at conception. Happily the scientists made the discovery.

It was the pall. At the end of three hours it was known that the death sheet was spreading out over Oakland. We may thank our stars that it was learned so early. Had the real warning come a few hours later the death list would have been appalling.

A new element had been discovered; or if not a new element, at least something which was tipping over all the laws of the atmospheric envelope. A new combination that was fatal. When the news and the warning went out, panic fell upon the bay shore.

But some men stuck. In the face of such terror there were those who stayed and with grimness and sacrifice hung to their posts for mankind. There are some who had said that the stuff of heroes had passed away. Let them then consider the case of John Robinson.

Robinson was a telegraph operator. Until that day he was a poor unknown; not a whit better than his fellows. Now he has a name that will run in history. In the face of what he knew he remained under the blanket. The last words out of Oakland—his last message:

"Whole city of Oakland in grip of strange madness. Keep out of Oakland,"—following which came a haphazard personal commentary:

"I can feel it coming on myself. It is like what our ancestors must have felt when they were getting drunk—alternating desires of fight and singing—a strange sensation, light, and ecstatic with a spasmodic twitching over the forehead. Terribly thirsty. Will stick it out if I can get enough water. Never so dry in my life."

Followed a lapse of silence. Then the last words: "I guess we're done for. There is some poison in the atmosphere—something. It has leaked, of course, out of this thing at Fourteenth and Broadway. Dr. Manson of the American Institute says it is something new that is forming a fatal combination; but he cannot understand a new element; the quantity is too enormous.

"Populace has been warned out of the city. All roads are packed with refugees. The Berkeley Hills are covered as with flies—north, east, and south and on the boats to Frisco. The poison, whatever it is, is advancing in a ring from Fourteenth and Broadway. You have got to pass it to these old boys of science. They are staying with that ring. Already they have calculated the rate of its advance and have given warning. They don't know what it is, but they have figured just how fast it is moving. They have saved the city.

"I am one of the few men now inside the wave. Out of curiosity I have stuck. I have a jug and as long as it lasts I shall stay. Strange feeling. Dry, dry, dry, as if the juice of one's life cells was turning into dust. Water evaporating almost instantly. It cannot pass through glass. Whatever the poison it has an affinity for moisture. Do not understand it. I have had enough—"

That was all. After that there was no more news out of Oakland. It is the only word that we have out of the pall itself. It was short and disconnected and a bit slangy; but for all that a basis from which to conjecture.

It is a strange and glorious thing how some men will stick to the post of danger. This operator knew that it meant death; but he held with duty. Had he been a man of scientific training his information might have been of incalculable value. However, may God bless his heroic soul!

What we know is thirst! The word that came from the experts confirmed it. Some new element of force was stealing or sapping the humidity out of the atmosphere. Whether this was combining and entering into a poison could not be determined.

Chemists worked frantically at the outposts of the advancing ring. In four hours it had covered the city; in six it had reached San Leandro, and was advancing on toward Haywards.

It was a strange story and incredible from the beginning. No wonder the world doubted. Such a thing had never happened. We had accepted the law of judging the future by the past; by deduction; we were used to sequence and to law; to the laws of Nature. This thing did look like a miracle; which was merely because—as usually it is with "miracles"—we could not understand it. Happily, we can look back now and still place our faith in Nature.

The world doubted and was afraid. Was this peril to spread

slowly over the whole state of California and then on to the—world. Doubt always precedes terror. A tense world waited. Then came the word of reassurance—from the scientists:

"Danger past; vigor of the ring is abating. Calculation has deduced that the wave is slowly decreasing in potentiality. It is too early yet to say that there will be recessions, as the wave is just reaching its zenith. What it is we cannot say; but it cannot be inexplicable. After a little time it will all be explained. Say to the world there is no cause for alarm."

But the world was now aroused; as it doubted the truth before, it doubted now the reassurance. Did the scientists know? Could they have only seen the future! We know now that they did not. There was but one man in all the world great enough to foresee disaster. That man was Charley Huyck.

# 3

# THE MOUNTAIN THAT WAS

On the same day on which all this happened, a young man, Pizzozi by name and of Italian parentage, left the little town of Ione in Amador County, California, with a small truck-load of salt. He was one of the cattlemen whose headquarters or home-farms are clustered about the foothills of the Sierras. In the wet season they stay with their home-land in the valley, in the summer they penetrate into the mountains. Pizzozi had driven in from the mountains the night before, after salt. He had been on the road since midnight.

Two thousand salt-hungry cattle do not allow time for gossip. With the thrift of his race, Joe had loaded up his truck and after a running snatch at breakfast was headed back into the mountains. When the news out of Oakland was thrilling around the world he was far into the Sierras.

The summer quarters of Pizzozi were close to Mt. Heckla, whose looming shoulders rose square in the center of the pasture of the three brothers. It was not a noted mountain—that is, until this day—and had no reason for a name other than that it was a peak outstanding from the range; like a thousand others, rugged, pine clad, coated with deer-brush, red soil, and mountain miserie.

It was the deer-brush that gave it value to the Pizzozis—a succulent feed richer than alfalfa. In the early summer they would come up with bony cattle. When they returned in the fall they went out driving beef-steaks. But inland cattle must have more than forage. Salt is the tincture that makes them healthy.

It was far past the time of the regular salting. Pizzozi was in a hurry. It was nine o'clock when he passed through the mining town of Jackson; and by twelve o'clock—the minute of the disaster—he was well beyond the last little hamlet that linked up with civilization. It was four o'clock when he drew up at the little pine-sheltered cabin that was his headquarters for the summer.

He had been on the road since midnight. He was tired. The long weary hours of driving, the grades, the unvaried stress though the deep red dust, the heat, the stretch of a night and day had worn both mind and muscle. It had been his turn to go after salt; now that he was here, he could lie in for a bit of rest while his brothers did the salting.

It was a peaceful spot! this cabin of the Pizzozis; nestled among the virgin shade trees, great tall feathery sugar-pines with a mountain live oak spreading over the door yard. To the east the rising heights of the Sierras, misty, gray-green, undulating into the distance to the pink-white snow crests of Little Alpine. Below in the canyon, the waters of the Mokolumne; to the west the heavy dark masses of Mt. Heckla, deep verdant in the cool of coming evening.

Joe drew up under the shade of the live oak. The air was full of cool, sweet scent of the afternoon. No moment could have been more peaceful; the blue clear sky overhead, the breath of summer, and the soothing spice of the pine trees. A shepherd dog came bounding from the doorway to meet him.

It was his favorite cow dog. Usually when Joe came back the dog would be far down the road to forestall him. He had wondered, absently, coming up, at the dog's delay. A dog is most of all a creature of habit; only something unusual would detain him. However the dog was here; as the man drew up he rushed out to greet him. A rush, a circle, a bark, and a whine of welcome. Perhaps the dog had been asleep.

But Joe noticed that whine; he was wise in the ways of dogs; when Ponto whined like that there was something unusual. It was not effusive or spontaneous; but rather of the delight of succor. After scarce a minute of petting, the dog squatted and faced to the westward. His whine was startling; almost fearful.

Pizzozi knew that something was wrong. The dog drew up, his stub tail erect, and his hair all bristled; one look was for his master and the other whining and alert to Mt. Heckla. Puzzled, Joe gazed at the mountain. But he saw nothing.

Was it the canine instinct, or was it coincidence? We have the account from Pizzozi. From the words of the Italian, the dog was afraid. It was not the way of Ponto; usually in the face of danger he was alert and eager; now he drew away to the cabin. Joe wondered.

Inside the shack he found nothing but evidence of departure. There was no sign of his brothers. It was his turn to go to sleep; he was wearied almost to numbness, for forty-eight hours he had not closed an eyelid. On the table were a few unwashed dishes and crumbs of eating. One of the three rifles that hung usually on the wall was missing; the coffee pot was on the floor with the lid open. On the bed the coverlets were mussed up. It was a temptation to go to sleep. Back of him the open door and Ponto. The whine of the dog drew his will and his consciousness into correlation. A faint rustle in the sugar-pines soughed from the canyon.

Joe watched the dog. The sun was just glowing over the crest of the mountain; on the western line the deep lacy silhouettes of the pine trees and the bare bald head of Heckla. What was it? His brothers should be on hand for the salting; it was not their custom to put things off for the morrow. Shading his eyes he stepped out of the doorway.

The dog rose stealthily and walked behind him, uneasily, with the same insistent whine and ruffled hair. Joe listened. Only the mountain murmurs, the sweet breath of the forest, and in the lapse of bated breath the rippling melody of the river far below him.

"What you see, Ponto? What you see?"

At the words the dog sniffed and advanced slightly—a growl and then a sudden scurry to the heels of his master. Ponto was afraid. It puzzled Pizzozi. But whatever it was that roused his fear, it was on Mt. Heckla.

This is one of the strange parts of the story—the part the dog played, and what came after. Although it is a trivial thing it is one of the most inexplicable. Did the dog sense it? We have no measure for the range of instinct, but we do have it that before the destruction of Pompeii the beasts roared in their cages. Still, knowing what we now know, it is hard to accept the analogy. It may, after all have been coincidence.

Nevertheless it decided Pizzozi. The cattle needed salt. He would catch up his pinto and ride over to the salt logs.

There is no moment in the cattle industry quite like the salting on the range. It is not the most spectacular perhaps, but surely it is not lacking in intenseness. The way of Pizzozi was musical even if not operatic. He had a long-range call, a rising rhythm that for depth and tone had a peculiar effect on the shattered stillness. It echoed and reverberated, and pealed from the top to the bottom of the mountain. The salt call is the talisman of the mountains.

"*Alleewahoo!*"

Two thousand cattle augmented by a thousand strays held up their heads in answer. The sniff of the welcome salt call! Through the whole range of the man's voice the stock stopped in their leafy pasture and listened.

"*Alleewahoo!*"

An old cow bellowed. It was the beginning of bedlam. From the bottom of the mountain to the top and for miles beyond went forth the salt call. Three thousand head bellowed to the delight of salting.

Pizzozi rode along. Each lope of his pinto through the tall tangled miserie was accented. "*Alleewahoo! Alleewahoo!*" The rending of brush, the confusion, and pandemonium spread to the very bottom of the leafy gulches. It is no place for a pedestrian. Heads and tails erect, the cattle were stampeding toward the logs.

A few head had beat him to it. These he quickly drove away and cut the sack open. With haste he poured it upon the logs; then he rode out of the dust that for yards about the place was tramped to the finest powder. The center of a herd of salting range stock is no place for comfort. The man rode away; to the left he ascended a low knob where he would be safe from the stampede; but close enough to distinguish the brands.

In no time the place was alive with milling stock. Old cows, heifers, bulls, calves, steers rushed out of the crashing brush into the clearing. There is no moment exactly like it. What before had been a broad clearing of brownish reddish dust was trampled into a vast cloud of bellowing blur, a thousand cattle, and still coming. From the farthest height came the echoing call. Pizzozi glanced up at the top of the mountain.

And then a strange thing happened.

From what we gathered from the excited accounts of Pizzozi it was instantaneous; and yet by the same words it was of such a peculiar and beautiful effect as never to be forgotten. A bluish azure shot though with a myriad flecks of crimson, a peculiar vividness of opalescence; the whole world scintillating; the sky, the air, the mountain, a vast flame of color so wide and so intense that there seemed not a thing beside it. And instantaneous—it was over almost before it was started. No noise or warning, and no subsequent detonation: as silent as winking and much, indeed, like the queer blur of color induced by defective vision. All in the fraction of a second. Pizzozi had been gazing at the mountain. There was no mountain!

Neither were there cattle. Where before had been the shade of the towering peak was now the rays of the western sun. Where had been the blur of the milling herd and its deafening pandemonium was now a strange silence. The transparency of the air was unbroken into the distance. Far off lay a peaceful range in the sunset. There was no mountain! Neither were there cattle!

For a moment the man had enough to do with his plunging mustang. In the blur of the subsequent second Pizzozi remembers nothing but a convulsion of fighting horseflesh bucking, twisting, plunging, the gentle pinto suddenly maddened into a demon. It required all the skill of the cowman to retain his saddle.

He did not know that he was riding on the rim of Eternity. In his mind was the dim subconscious realization of a thing that had happened. In spite of all his efforts the horse fought backward. It was some moments before he conquered. Then he looked.

It was a slow, hesitant moment. One cannot account for what he will do in the open face of a miracle. What the Italian beheld was enough for terror. The sheer immensity of the thing was too much for thinking.

At the first sight his simplex mind went numb from sheer impotence; his terror to a degree frozen. The whole of Mt. Heckla had been shorn away; in the place of its darkened shadow the sinking sun was blinking in his face; the whole western sky all golden. There was no vestige of the flat salt-clearing at the base of the mountain. Of the two thousand cattle milling in the dust not a one remained. The man crossed himself in stupor. Mechanically he put the spurs to the pinto.

But the mustang would not. Another struggle with bucking, fighting, maddened horseflesh. The cowman must needs bring in all the skill of his training; but by the time he had conquered his mind had settled within some scope of comprehension.

The pony had good reasons for his terror. This time though the man's mind reeled it did not go dumb at the clash of immensity. Not only had the whole mountain been torn away, but its roots as well. The whole thing was up-side down; the world torn to its entrails. In place of what had been the height was a gulf so deep that its depths were blackness.

He was standing on the brink. He was a cool man, was Pizzozi; but it was hard in the confusion of such a miracle to think clearly; much less to reason. The prancing mustang was snorting with terror. The man glanced down.

The very dizziness of the gulf, sheer, losing itself into shadows and chaos overpowered him, his mind now clear enough for perception reeled at the distance. The depth was nauseating. His whole body succumbed to a sudden qualm of weakness: the sickness that comes just before falling. He went limp in the saddle.

But the horse fought backward; warned by instinct it drew back from the sheer banks of the gulf. It had no reason but its nature. At the instant it sensed the snapping of the iron will of its master. In a moment it had turned and was racing on its wild way out of the mountains. At supreme moments a cattle horse will always hit for home. The pinto and its limp rider were fleeing on the road to Jackson.

Pizzozi had no knowledge of what had occurred in Oakland. To him the whole thing had been but a flash of miracle; he could not reason. He did not curb his horse. That he was still in the saddle was due more to the near-instinct of his training than to his volition.

He did not even draw up at the cabin. That he could make better time with his motor than with his pinto did not occur to him; his mind was far too busy; and, now that the thing was passed, too full of terror. It was forty-four miles to town; it was night and the stars were shining when he rode into Jackson.

# 4

## "MAN—A GREAT LITTLE BUG"

And what of Charley Huyck? It was his anticipation, and his training which leaves us here to tell the story. Were it not for the strange manner of his rearing, and the keen faith and appreciation of Dr. Robold there would be to-day no tale to tell. The little incident of the burning glass had grown. If there is no such thing as Fate there is at least something that comes very close to being Destiny.

On this night we find Charley at the observatory in Arizona. He is a grown man and a great one, and though mature not so very far drawn from the lad we met on the street selling papers. Tall, slender, very slightly stooped and with the same idealistic, dreaming eyes of the poet. Surely no one at first glance would have taken him for a scientist. Which he was and was not.

Indeed, there is something vastly different about the science of Charley Huyck. Science to be sure, but not prosaic. He was the first and perhaps the last of the school of Dr. Robold, a peculiar combination of poetry and fact, a man of vision, of vast, far-seeing faith and idealism linked and based on the coldest and sternest truths of materialism. A peculiar tenet of the theory of Robold: "True science to be itself should be half poetry." Which any of us who have read or been at school know it is not. It is a peculiar theory and though rather wild still with some points in favor.

We all of us know our schoolmasters; especially those of science and what they stand for. Facts, facts, nothing but facts; no dreams or romance. Looking back we can grant them just about the emotions of cucumbers. We remember their cold, hard features, the prodding after fact, the accumulation of data. Surely there is no poetry in them.

Yet we must not deny that they have been by far the most potent of all men in the progress of civilization. Not even Robold would deny it.

The point is this:

The doctor maintained that from the beginning the progress of material civilization had been along three distinct channels; science, invention, and administration. It was simply his theory that the first two should be one; that the scientist deal not alone with dry fact but with invention, and that the inventor, unless he is a scientist, has mastered but half his trade. "The really great scientist should be a visionary," said Robold, "and an inventor is merely a poet, with tools."

Which is where we get Charley Huyck. He was a visionary, a scientist, a poet with tools, the protege of Dr. Robold. He dreamed things that no scientist had thought of. And we are thankful for his dreaming.

The one great friend of Huyck was Professor Williams, a man from Charley's home city, who had known him even back in the days of selling papers. They had been cronies in boyhood, in their teens, and again at College. In after years, when Huyck had become the visionary, the mysterious Man of the Mountain, and Williams a great professor of astronomy, the friendship was as strong as ever.

But there was a difference between them. Williams was exact to acuteness, with not a whit of vision beyond pure science. He had been reared in the old stone-cold theory of exactness; he lived in figures. He could not understand Huyck or his reasoning. Perfectly willing to follow as far as facts permitted he refused to step off into speculation.

Which was the point between them. Charley Huyck had vision; although exact as any man, he had ever one part of his mind soaring out into speculation. What is, and what might be, and the gulf between. To bridge the gulf was the life work of Charley Huyck.

In the snug little office in Arizona we find them; Charley with his feet poised on the desk and Williams precise and punctilious, true to his training, defending the exactness of his philosophy. It was the cool of the evening; the sun was just mellowing the heat of the desert. Through the open door and windows a cool wind was blowing. Charley was smoking; the same old pipe had been the bane of Williams's life at college.

"Then we know?" he was asking.

"Yes," spoke the professor, "what we know, Charley, we know; though of course it is not much. It is very hard, nay impossible, to deny figures. We have not only the proofs of geology but of astronomical calculation, we have facts and figures plus our sidereal relations all about us.

"The world must come to an end. It is a hard thing to say it, but it is a fact of science. Slowly, inevitably, ruthlessly, the end will come. A mere question of arithmetic."

Huyck nodded. It was his special function in life to differ with his former roommate. He had come down from his own mountain in Colorado just for the delight of difference.

"I see. Your old calculations of tidal retardation. Or if that doesn't work the loss of oxygen and the water."

"Either one or the other; a matter of figures; the earth is being drawn every day by the sun: its rotation is slowing up; when the time comes it will act to the sun in exactly the same manner as the moon acts to the earth to-day."

"I understand. It will be a case of eternal night for one side of the earth, and eternal day for the other. A case of burn up or freeze up."

"Exactly. Of if it doesn't reach to that, the water gas will gradually lose out into sidereal space and we will go to desert. Merely a question of the old dynamical theory of gases; of the molecules to be in motion, to be forever colliding and shooting out into variance.

"Each minute, each hour, each day we are losing part of our atmospheric envelope. In course of time it will all be gone; when it is we shall be all desert. For instance, take a look outside. This is Arizona. Once it was the bottom of a deep blue sea. Why deny when we can already behold the beginning."

The other laughed.

"Pretty good mathematics at that, professor. Only—"

"Only?"

"That it is merely mathematics."

"Merely mathematics?" The professor frowned slightly. "Mathematics do not lie, Charlie, you cannot get away from them. What sort of fanciful argument are you bringing up now?"

"Simply this," returned the other, "that you depend too much on figures. They are material and in the nature of things can only be employed in a calculation of what may happen in the future. You must have premises to stand on, facts. Your figures are rigid: they have no elasticity; unless your foundations are permanent and faultless your deductions will lead you only into error."

"Granted; just the point: we know where we stand. Wherein are we in error?"

It was the old point of difference. Huyck was ever crashing down the idols of pure materialism. Williams was of the world-wide school.

"You are in error, my dear professor, in a very little thing and a very large one."

"What is that?"

"Man."

"Man?"

"Yes. He's a great little bug. You have left him out of your calculation—which he will upset."

The professor smiled indulgently. "I'll allow; he is at least a conceited bug; but you surely cannot grant him much when pitted against the Universe."

"No? Did it ever occur to you. Professor, what the Universe is? The stars for instance? Space, the immeasurable distance of Infinity. Have you never dreamed?"

Williams could not quite grasp him. Huyck had a habit that had grown out of childhood. Always he would allow his opponent to commit himself. The professor did not answer. But the other spoke.

"Ether. You know it. Whether mind or granite. For instance, your desert." He placed his finger to his forehead. "Your mind, my mind—localized ether."

"What are you driving at?"

"Merely this. Your universe has intelligence. It has mind as well as matter. The little knot called the earth is becoming conscious. Your deductions are incompetent unless they embrace mind as well as matter, and they cannot do it. Your mathematics are worthless."

The professor bit his lip.

"Always fanciful." he commented, "and visionary. Your argument is beautiful, Charley, and hopeful. I would that it were true. But all things must mature. Even an earth must die."

"Not our earth. You look into the past, professor, for your proof, and I look into the future. Give a planet long enough time in maturing and it will develop life; give it still longer and it will produce intelligence. Our own earth is just coming into consciousness; it has thirty million years, at least, to run."

"You mean?"

"This. That man is a great little bug. Mind: the intelligence of the earth."

This of course is a bit dry. The conversation of such men very often is to those who do not care to follow them. But it is very pertinent to what came after. We know now, everyone knows, that Charley Huyck was right. Even Professor Williams admits it. Our earth is conscious. In less than twenty-four hours it had to employ its consciousness to save itself from destruction.

A bell rang. It was the private wire that connected the office with the residence. The professor picked up the receiver. "Just a minute. Yes? All right." Then to his companion: "I must go over to the house, Charley. We have plenty of time. Then we can go up to the observatory."

Which shows how little we know about ourselves. Poor Professor Williams! Little did he think that those casual words were the last he would ever speak to Charley Huyck.

The whole world seething! The beginning of the end! Charley Huyck in the vortex. The next few hours were to be the most strenuous of the planet's history.

# 5

# APPROACHING DISASTER

It was night. The stars which had just been coming out were spotted by millions over the sleeping desert. One of the nights that are peculiar to the country, which we all of us know so well, if not from experience, at least from hearsay; mellow, soft, sprinkled like salted fire, twinkling.

Each little light a message out of infinity. Cosmic grandeur; mind: chaos, eternity—a night for dreaming. Whoever had chosen the spot in the desert had picked full well. Charley had spoken of consciousness. On that night when he gazed up at the stars he was its personification. Surely a good spirit was watching over the earth.

A cool wind was blowing; on its breath floated the murmurs from the village; laughter, the song of children, the purring of motors and the startled barking of a dog; the confused drone of man and his civilization. From the eminence the observatory looked down upon the town and the sheen of light, spotting like jewels in the dim glow of the desert. To the east the mellow moon just tipping over the mountain. Charley stepped to the window.

He could see it all. The subtle beauty that was so akin to poetry: the stretch of desert, the mountains, the light in the eastern sky; the dull level shadow that marked the plain to the northward. To the west the mountains looming black to the star line. A beautiful night; sweetened with the breath of desert and tuned to its slumber.

Across the lawn he watched the professor descending the pathway under the acacias. An automobile was coming up the driveway; as it drove up under the arcs he noticed its powerful lines and its driver; one of those splendid pleasure cars that have returned to favor during the last decade; the soft purr of its motor, the great heavy tires and its coating of dust. There is a lure about a great car coming in from the desert. The car stopped, Charley noted. Doubtless some one for Williams. If it were, he would go into the observatory alone.

In the strict sense of the word Huyck was not an astronomer. He had not made it his profession. But for all that he knew things about the stars that the more exact professors had not dreamed of. Charley was a dreamer. He had a code all his own and a manner of reasoning. Between him and the stars lay a secret.

He had not divulged it, or if he had, it was in such an open way that it was laughed at. It was not cold enough in calculation or, even if so, was too far from their deduction. Huyck had imagination; his universe was alive and potent; it had intelligence. Matter could not live without it. Man was its manifestation; just come to consciousness. The universe teemed with intelligence. Charley looked at the stars.

He crossed the office, passed through the reception-room

and thence to the stairs that led to the observatory. In the time that would lapse before the coming of his friend he would have ample time for observation. Somehow he felt that there was time for discovery. He had come down to Arizona to employ the lens of his friend the astronomer. The instrument that he had erected on his own mountain in Colorado had not given him the full satisfaction that he expected. Here in Arizona, in the dry clear air, which had hitherto given such splendid results, he hoped to find what he was after. But little did he expect to discover the terrible thing he did.

It is one of the strangest parts of the story that he should be here at the very moment when Fate and the world's safety would have had him. For years he and Dr. Robold had been at work on their visionary projects. They were both dreamers. While others had scoffed they had silently been at their great work on kinetics.

The boy and the burning glass had grown under the tutelage of Dr. Robold: the time was about at hand when he could out-rival the saying of Archimedes. Though the world knew it not, Charley Huyck had arrived at the point where he could literally burn up the earth.

But he was not sinister; though he had the power he had of course not the slightest intention. He was a dreamer and it was part of his dream that man break his thraldom to the earth and reach out into the universe. It was a great conception and were it not for the terrible event which took his life we have no doubt but that he would have succeeded.

It was ten-thirty when he mounted the steps and seated himself. He glanced at his watch: he had a good ten minutes. He had computed before just the time for the observation. For months he had waited for just this moment; he had not hoped to be alone and now that he was in solitary possession he counted himself fortunate. Only the stars and Charley Huyck knew the secret; and not even he dreamed what it would amount to.

From his pocket he drew a number of papers; most of them covered with notations; some with drawings; and a good sized map in colors. This he spread before him, and with his pencil began to draw right across its face a net of lines and cross lines. A number of figures and a rapid computation. He nodded and then he made the observation.

It would have been interesting to study the face of Charley Huyck during the next few moments. At first he was merely receptive, his face placid but with the studious intentness of one who has come to the moment: and as he began to find what he was after—an eagerness of satisfaction. Then a queer blankness; the slight movement of his body stopped, and the tapping of his feet ceased entirely.

For a full five minutes an absolute intentness. During that time he was out among the stars beholding what not even he had dreamed of. It was more than a secret: and what it was only Charley Huyck of all the millions of men could have recognized. Yet it was more than even he had expected. When he at last drew away his face was chalk-like; great drops of sweat stood on his forehead: and the terrible truth in his eyes made him look ten years older.

"My God!"

For a moment indecision and strange impotence. The truth he had beheld numbed action; from his lips the mumbled words:

"This world; my world; our great and splendid mankind!"

A sentence that was despair and a benediction.

Then mechanically he turned back to confirm his observation. This time, knowing what he would see, he was not so horrified: his mind was cleared by the plain fact of what he was beholding. When at last he drew away his face was settled.

He was a man who thought quickly—thank the stars for that—and, once he thought, quick to spring to action. There was a peril poising over the earth. If it were to be voided there was not a second to lose in weighing up the possibilities.

He had been dreaming all his life. He had never thought that the climax was to be the very opposite of what he hoped for. In his under mind he prayed for Dr. Robold—dead and gone forever. Were he only here to help him!

He seized a piece of paper. Over its white face he ran a mass of computations. He worked like lightning; his fingers plying and his mind keyed to the pin-point of genius. Not one thing did he overlook in his calculation. If the earth had a chance he would find it.

There are always possibilities. He was working out the odds of the greatest race since creation. While the whole world slept, while the uncounted millions lay down in fond security, Charley Huyck there in the lonely room on the desert drew out their figured odds to the point of infinity.

"Just one chance in a million."

He was going to take it. The words were not out of his mouth before his long legs were leaping down the stairway. In the flash of seconds his mind was rushing into clear action. He had had years of dreaming; all his years of study and tutelage under Robold gave him just the training for such a disaster.

But he needed time. Time! Time! Why was it so precious? He must get to his own mountain. In six jumps he was in the office.

It was empty. The professor had not returned. He thought rather grimly and fleetingly of their conversation a few minutes before; what would Williams think now of science and consciousness? He picked up the telephone receiver. While he waited he saw out of the corner of his eye the car in the driveway. It was—

"Hello. The professor? What? Gone down to town? No! Well, say, this is Charley"—he was watching the car in front of the building. "Say, hello—tell him I have gone home, home! H-o-m-e to Colorado—to Colorado, yes—to the mountain—the m-o-u-n-t-a-i-n. Oh, never mind—I'll leave a note."

He clamped down the receiver. On the desk he scrawled on a piece of paper:

Ed:

"Look these up. I'm bound for the mountain. No time to explain. There's a car outside. Stay with the lens. Don't leave it. If the earth goes up you will know that I have not reached the mountain."

Beside the note he placed one of the maps that he had in his pocket—with his pencil drew a black cross just above the center. Under the map were a number of computations.

It is interesting to note that in the stress of the great critical moment he forgot the professor's title. It was a good thing. When Williams read it he recognized the significance. All through their life in crucial moments he had been "Ed." to Charley.

But the note was all he was destined to find. A brisk wind was blowing. By a strange balance of fate the same movement that let Huyck out of the building ushered in the wind and upset calculation.

It was a little thing, but it was enough to keep all the world in ignorance and despair. The eddy whisking in through the door picked up the precious map, poised it like a tiny plane, and dropped it neatly behind a bookcase.

# 6

# A RACE TO SAVE THE WORLD

Huyck was working in a straight line. Almost before his last words on the phone were spoken he had requisitioned that automobile outside; whether money or talk, faith or force, he was going to have it. The hum of the motor sounded in his ears as he ran down the steps. He was hatless and in his shirt-sleeves. The driver was just putting some tools in the car. With one jump Charley had him by the collar.

"Five thousand dollars if you can get me to Robold Mountain in twenty hours."

The very suddenness of the rush caught the man by surprise and lurched him against the car, turning him half around. Charley found himself gazing into dull brown eyes and sardonic laughter: a long, thin nose and lips drooped at the corners, then as suddenly tipping up—a queer creature, half devil, half laughter, and all fun.

"Easy, Charley, easy! How much did you say? Whisper it."

It was Bob Winters. Bob Winters and his car. And waiting.

Surely no twist of fortune could have been greater. He was a college chum of Huyck's and of the professor's. If there was one man that could make the run in the time allotted, Bob was he. But Huyck was impersonal. With the burden on his mind he thought of naught but his destination.

"Ten thousand!" he shouted.

The man held back his head. Huyck was far too serious to appreciate mischief. But not the man.

"Charley Huyck, of all men. Did young Lochinvar come out of the West? How much did you say? This desert air and the dust, 'tis hard on the hearing. She must be a young, fair maiden. Ten thousand."

"Twenty thousand. Thirty thousand. Damnation, man, you can have the mountain. Into the car."

By sheer subjective strength he forced the other into the machine. It was not until they were shooting out of the grounds on two wheels that he realized that the man was Bob Winters. Still the workings of fate.

The madcap and wild Bob of the races! Surely Destiny was on the job. The challenge of speed and the premium. At the opportune moment before disaster the two men were brought together. Minutes weighed up with centuries and hours outbalanced millenniums. The whole world slept; little did it dream that its very life was riding north with these two men into the midnight.

Into the midnight! The great car, the pride of Winter's heart, leaped between the pillars. At the very outset, madcap that he was, he sent her into seventy miles an hour; they fairly jumped off the hill into the village. At a full seventy-five he took the curve; she skidded, sheered half around and swept on.

For an instant Charley held his breath. But the master hand held her; she steadied, straightened, and shot out into the desert. Above the whir of the motor, flying dust and blurring what-not, Charley got the tones of his companion's voice. He had heard the words somewhere in history.

"Keep your seat, Mr. Greely. Keep your seat!"

The moon was now far up over the mountain, the whole desert was bathed in a mellow twilight; in the distance the mountains brooded like an uncertain slumbering cloud bank. They were headed straight to the northward; though there was a better road round about. Winters had chosen the hard, rocky bee-line to the mountain.

He knew Huyck and his reputation; when Charley offered thirty thousand for a twenty-hour drive it was not mere byplay. He had happened in at the observatory to drop in on Williams on his way to the coast. They had been classmates; likewise he and Charley.

When the excited man out of the observatory had seized him by the collar, Winters merely had laughed. He was the speed king. The three boys who had gone to school were now playing with the destiny of the earth. But only Huyck knew it.

Winters wondered. Through miles and miles of fleeting sagebrush, cacti and sand and desolation, he rolled over the problem. Steady as a rock, slightly stooped, grim and as certain as steel he held to the north. Charley Huyck by his side, hatless, coatless, his hair dancing to the wind, all impatience. Why was it? Surely a man even for death would have time to get his hat.

The whole thing spelled speed to Bob Winters; perhaps it was the infusion of spirit or the intensity of his companion; but the thrill ran into his vitals. Thirty thousand dollars—for a stake like that—what was the balance? He had been called Wild Bob for his daring; some had called him insane; on this night his insanity was enchantment.

It was wild; the lee of the giant roadster a whirring shower of gravel: into the darkness, into the night the car fought over the distance. The terrific momentum and the friction of the air fought in their faces; Huyck's face was unprotected: in no time his lips were cracked, and long before they had crossed the level his whole face was bleeding.

But he heeded it not. He only knew that they were moving; that slowly, minute by minute, they were cutting down the odds that bore disaster. In his mind a maze of figures; the terrible sight he had seen in the telescope and the thing impending. Why had he kept his secret?

Over and again he impeached himself and Dr. Robold. It had come to this. The whole world sleeping and only himself to save it. Oh, for a few minutes, for one short moment! Would he get it?

At last they reached the mountains. A rough, rocky road, and but little traveled. Happily Winters had made it once before, and knew it. He took it with every bit of speed they could stand, but even at that it was diminished to a minimum.

For hours they fought over grades and gulches, dry washouts and boulders. It was dawn, and the sky was growing pink when they rode down again upon the level. It was here that they ran across their first trouble; and it was here that Winters began to realize vaguely what a race they might be running.

The particular level which they had entered was an elbow of the desert projecting into the mountains just below a massive, newly constructed dam. The reservoir had but lately been filled, and all was being put in readiness for the dedication.

An immense sheet of water extending far back into the mountains—it was intended before long to transform the desert into a garden. Below, in the valley, was a town, already the center of a prosperous irrigation settlement; but soon, with the added area, to become a flourishing city. The elbow, where they struck it, was perhaps twenty miles across. Their northward path would take them just outside the tip where the foothills of the opposite mountain chain melted into the desert. Without ado Winters put on all speed and plunged across the sands. And then:

It was much like winking; but for all that something far more impressive. To Winters, on the left hand of the car and with the east on the right hand, it was much as if the sun had suddenly leaped up and as suddenly plumped down behind the horizon—a vast vividness of scintillating opalescence: an azure, flaming diamond shot by a million fire points.

Instantaneous and beautiful. In the pale dawn of the desert air its wonder and color were beyond all beauty. Winters caught it out of the corner of his eye; it was so instantaneous and so illusive that he was not certain. Instinctively he looked to his companion.

But Charley, too, had seen it. His attitude of waiting and hoping was vigorized into vivid action. He knew just what it was. With one hand he clutched Winters and fairly shouted.

"On, on, Bob! On, as you value your life. Put into her every bit of speed you have got."

At the same instant, at the same breath came a roar that was not to be forgotten; crunching, rolling, terrible—like the mountain moving.

Bob knew it. It was the dam. Something had broken it. To the east the great wall of water fall-out of the mountains! A beautiful sight and terrible; a relentless glassy roller fringed along its base by a lace of racing foam. The upper part was as smooth as crystal; the stored-up waters of the mountain moving out compactly. The man thought of the little town below and its peril. But Huyck thought also. He shouted in Winter's ear:

"Never mind the town. Keep straight north. Over yonder

to the point of the water. The town will have to drown."

It was inexorable; there was no pity; the very strength and purpose of the command drove into the other's understanding. Dimly now he realized that they were really running a race against time. Winters was a daredevil; the very catastrophe sent a thrill of exultation through him. It was the climax, the great moment of his life, to be driving at a hundred miles an hour under that wall of water.

The roar was terrible. Before they were half across it seemed to the two men that the very sound would drown them. There was nothing in the world but pandemonium. The strange flash was forgotten in the terror of the living wall that was reaching out to engulf them. Like insects they whizzed in the open face of the deluge. When they had reached the tip they were so close that the outrunning fringe of the surf was at their wheels.

Around the point with the wide open plain before them. With the flood behind them it was nothing to outrun it. The waters with a wider stretch spread out. In a few moments they had left all behind them.

But Winters wondered; what was the strange flash of evanescent beauty? He knew this dam and its construction; to outlast the centuries. It had been whiffed in a second. It was not lightning. He had heard no sound other than the rush of the waters. He looked to his companion.

Hucyk nodded.

"That's the thing we are racing. We have only a few hours. Can we make it?"

Bob had thought that he was getting all the speed possible out of his motor. What it yielded from that moment on was a revelation.

It is not safe and hardly possible to be driving at such speed on the desert. Only the best car and a firm roadway can stand it. A sudden rut, squirrel hole, or pocket of sand is as good as destruction. They rushed on till noon.

Not even Winters, with all his alertness, could avoid it. Perhaps he was weary. The tedious hours, the racking speed had worn him to exhaustion. They had ceased to individualize, their way a blur, a nightmare of speed and distance.

It came suddenly, a blind barranca—one of those sunken, useless channels that are death to the unwary. No warning.

It was over just that quickly. A mere flash of consciousness plus a sensation of flying. Two men broken on the sands and the great, beautiful roadster a twisted ruin.

# 7

# A RIVEN CONTINENT

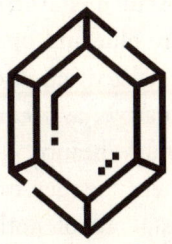

But back to the world. No one knew about Charley Huyck nor what was occurring on the desert. Even if we had it would have been impossible to construe connection.

After the news out of Oakland, and the destruction of Mt. Heckla, we were far too appalled. The whole thing was beyond us. Not even the scientists with all their data could find one thing to work on. The wires of the world buzzed with wonder and with panic. We were civilized. It is really strange how quickly, in spite of our boasted powers, we revert to the primitive.

Superstition cannot die. Where was no explanation must be miracle. The thing had been repeated. When would it strike again. And where?

There was not long to wait. But this time the stroke was of far more consequence and of far more terror. The sheer might of the thing shook the earth. Not a man or government that would not resign in the face of such destruction.

It was omnipotent. A whole continent had been riven. It would be impossible to give description of such catastrophe; no pen can tell it any more than it could describe the creation. We can only follow in its path.

On the morning after the first catastrophe, at eight o'clock, just south of the little city of Santa Cruz, on the north shore of the Bay of Monterey, the same light and the same, though not quite the same, instantaneousness. Those who beheld it report a vast ball of azure blue and opalescent fire and motion; a strange sensation of vitalized vibration; of personified living force. In shape like a marble, as round as a full moon in its glory, but of infinitely more beauty.

It came from nowhere; neither from above the earth nor below it. Seeming to leap out of nothing, it glided or rather vanished to the eastward. Still the effect of winking, though this time, perhaps from a distanced focus, more vivid. A dot or marble, like a full moon, burning, opal, soaring to the eastward.

And instantaneous. Gone as soon as it was come; noiseless and of phantom beauty; like a finger of the Omnipotent tracing across the world, and as terrible. The human mind had never conceived a thing so vast.

Beginning at the sands of the ocean the whole country had vanished; a chasm twelve miles wide and of unknown depth running straight to the eastward, where had been farms and homes was nothing; the mountains had been seared like butter. Straight as an arrow.

Then the roar of the deluge. The waters of the Pacific breaking through its sands and rolling into the Gulf of Mexico. That there was no heat was evidenced by the fact that there was no steam. The thing could not be internal. Yet what was it?

One can only conceive in figures. From the shores of Santa Cruz to the Atlantic—a few seconds; then out into the eastern ocean straight out into the Sea of the Sargasso. A great gulf riven straight across the face of North America.

The path seemed to follow the sun; it bore to the eastward with a slight southern deviation. The mountains it cut like cheese. Passing just north of Fresno it seared through the gigantic Sierras halfway between the Yosemite and Mt. Whitney, through the great desert to southern Nevada, thence across northern Arizona, New Mexico, Texas, Arkansas, Mississippi, Alabama, and Georgia, entering the Atlantic at a point halfway between Brunswick and Jacksonville. A great canal twelve miles in width linking the oceans. A cataclysmic blessing. Today, with thousands of ships bearing freight over its water, we can bless that part of the disaster.

But there was more to come. So far the miracle had been sporadic. Whatever had been its force it had been fatal only on point and occasion. In a way it had been local. The deadly atmospheric combination of its aftermath was invariable in its recession. There was no suffering. The death that it dealt was the death of obliteration. But now it entered on another stage.

The world is one vast ball, and, though large, still a very small place to live in. There are few of us, perhaps, who look upon it, or even stop to think of it, as a living being. Yet it is just that. It has its currents, life, pulse, and its fevers; it is coordinate; a million things such as the great streams of the ocean, the swirls of the atmosphere, make it a place to live in. And we are conscious only, or mostly, through disaster.

A strange thing happened.

The great opal like a mountain of fire had riven across the continent. From the beginning and with each succession the thing was magnified. But it was not until it had struck the waters of the Atlantic that we became aware of its full potency and its fatality.

The earth quivered at the shock, and man stood on his toes in terror. In twenty-four hours our civilization was literally falling to pieces. We were powerful with the forces that we understood; but against this that had been literally ripped from the unknown we were insignificant. The whole world was frozen. Let us see.

Into the Atlantic! The transition. Hitherto silence. But now the roar of ten thousand million Niagaras, the waters of the ocean rolling, catapulting, roaring into the gulf that had been seared in its bosom. The Gulf Stream cut in two, the currents that tempered our civilization sheared in a second. Straight into the Sargasso Sea. The great opal, liquid fire, luminescent, a ball like the setting sun, lay poised upon the ocean. It was the end of the earth!

What was this thing? The whole world knew of it in a second. And not a one could tell. In less than forty hours after its first appearance in Oakland it had consumed a mountain, riven a continent, and was drinking up an ocean. The tangled sea of the Sargasso, dead calm for ages, was a cataract; a swirling torrent of maddened waters rushed to the opal—and disappeared.

It was hellish and out of madness; as beautiful as it was uncanny. The high as the Himalayas brooding upon the water; its myriad colors blending, winking in a phantasm of iridescence. The beauty of its light could be seen a thousand miles. A thing out of mystery and out of forces. We had discovered many things and knew much; but had guessed no such thing as this. It was vampirish, and it was literally drinking up the earth.

Consequences were immediate. The point of contact was fifty miles across, the waters of the Atlantic with one accord turned to the magnet. The Gulf Stream veered straight from its course and out across the Atlantic. The icy currents from the poles freed from the warmer barrier descended along the coasts and thence out into the Sargasso Sea. The temperature of the temperate zone dipped below the point of a blizzard.

The first word come out of London. Freezing! And in July! The fruit and entire harvest of northern Europe destroyed. Olympic games at Copenhagen postponed by a foot of snow. The river Seine frozen. Snow falling in New York. Crops nipped with frost as far south as Cape Hatteras.

A fleet of airplanes was despatched from the United States and another from the west coast of Africa. Not half of them returned. Those that did reported even more disaster. The reports that were handed in were appalling. They had sailed straight on. It was like flying into the sun; the vividness of the opalescence was blinding, rising for miles above them alluring, drawing and unholy, and of a beauty that was terror.

Only the tardy had escaped. It even drew their motors, it was like gravity suddenly become vitalized and conscious. Thousands of machines vaulted into the opalescence. From those ahead hopelessly drawn and powerless came back the warning. But hundreds could not escape.

"Back," came the wireless. "Do not come too close. The thing is a magnet. Turn back before too late. Against this man is insignificant."

Then like gnats flitting into fire they vanished into the opalescence.

The others turned back. The whole world freezing shuddered in horror. A great vampire was brooding over the earth. The greatness that man had attained to was nothing. Civilization was tottering in a day. We were hopeless.

Then came the last revelation; the truth and verity of the disaster and the threatened climax. The water level of all the coast had gone down. Vast ebb tides had gone out not to return. Stretches of sand where had been surf extended far out into the sea. Then the truth! The thing, whatever it was, was drinking up the ocean.

# 8

# THE MAN WHO SAVED THE EARTH

It was tragic; grim, terrible, cosmic. Out of nowhere had come this thing that was eating up the earth. Not a thing out of all our science had there been to warn us; not a word from all our wise men. We who had built up our civilization, piece by piece, were after all but insects.

We were going out in a maze of beauty into the infinity whence we came. Hour by hour the great orb of opalescence grew in splendor; the effect and the beauty of its lure spread about the earth; thrilling, vibrant like suppressed music. The old earth helpless. Was it possible that out of her bosom she could not pluck one intelligence to save her? Was there not one law—no answer?

Out on the desert with his face to the sun lay the answer. Though almost hopeless there was still some time and enough of near-miracle to save us. A limping fate in the shape of two Indians and a battered runabout at the last moment.

Little did the two red men know the value of the two men found that day on the desert. To them the debris of the mighty car and the prone bodies told enough of the story. They were Samaritans; but there are many ages to bless them.

As it was there were many hours lost. Without this loss there would have been thousands spared and an almost immeasurable amount of disaster. But we have still to be thankful. Charley Huyck was still living.

He had been stunned; battered, bruised, and unconscious; but he had not been injured vitally. There was still enough left of him to drag himself to the old runabout and call for Winters. His companion, as it happened, was in even better shape than himself, and waiting. We do not know how they talked the red men out of their relic—whether by coaxing, by threat, or by force.

Straight north. Two men battered, worn, bruised, but steadfast, bearing in that limping old motorcar the destiny of the earth. Fate was still on the job, but badly crippled.

They had lost many precious hours. Winters had forfeited his right to the thirty thousand. He did not care. He understood vaguely that there was a stake over and above all money. Huyck said nothing; he was too maimed and too much below willpower to think of speaking. What had occurred during the many hours of their unconsciousness was unknown to them. It was not until they came sheer upon the gulf that had been riven straight across the continent that the awful truth dawned on them.

To Winters it was terrible. The mere glimpse of that blackened chasm was terror. It was bottomless; so deep that its depths were cloudy; the misty haze of its uncertain shadows was akin to chaos. He understood vaguely that it was related to that terrible thing they had beheld in the morning. It was not the power of man. Some force had been loosened which was ripping the earth to its vitals. Across the terror of the chasm he made out the dim outlines of the opposite wall. A full twelve miles across.

For a moment the sight overcame even Huyck himself. Full well he knew; but knowing, as he did, the full fact of the miracle was even more than he expected. His long years under Robold, his scientific imagination had given him comprehension. Not puny steam, nor weird electricity, but force, kinetics—out of the universe.

He knew. But knowing as he did, he was overcome by the horror. Such a thing turned loose upon the earth! He had lost many hours; he had but a few hours remaining. The thought gave him sudden energy. He seized Winters by the arm.

"To the first town, Bob. To the first town—an aerodome."

There was speed in that motor for all its decades. Winters turned about and shot out in a lateral course parallel to the great chasm. But for all his speed he could not keep back his question.

"In the name of Heaven, Charley, what did it? What is it?"

Came the answer; and it drove the lust of all speed through Winters:

"Bob," said Charley, "it is the end of the world—if we don't make it. But a few hours left. We must have an airplane. I must make the mountain."

It was enough for Wild Bob. He settled down. It was only an old runabout; but he could get speed out of a wheelbarrow. He had never driven a race like this. Just once did he speak. The words were characteristic.

"A world's record, Charley. And we're going to win. Just watch us."

And they did.

There was no time lost in the change. The mere fact of Huyck's name, his appearance and the manner of his arrival was enough. For the last hours messages had been pouring in at every post in the Rocky Mountains for Charley Huyck. After the failure of all others many thousands had thought of him.

Even the government, unappreciative before, had awakened to a belated and almost frantic eagerness. Orders were out that everything, no matter what, was to be at his disposal. He had been regarded as visionary; but in the face of what had occurred, visions were now the most practical things for mankind. Besides, Professor Williams had sent out to the world the strange portent of Huyck's note. For years there had been mystery on that mountain. Could it be?

Unfortunately we cannot give it the description we would like to give. Few men outside of the regular employees have ever been to the Mountain of Robold. From the very first, owing perhaps to the great forces stored, and the danger of carelessness, strangers and visitors had been barred. Then, too, the secrecy of Dr. Robold—and the respect of his successor. But we do know that the burning glass had grown into the mountain.

Bob Winters and the aviator are the only ones to tell us; the employees, one and all, chose to remain. The cataclysm that followed destroyed the work of Huyck and Robold—but not until it had served the greatest deed that ever came out of the minds of men. And had it not been for Huyck's insistence we would not have even the account that we are giving.

It was he who insisted, nay, begged, that his companions return while there was yet a chance. Full well he knew. Out of the universe, out of space he had coaxed the forces that would burn up the earth. The great ball of luminous opalescence, and the diminishing ocean!

There was but one answer. Through the imaginative genius

of Robold and Huyck, fate had worked up to the moment. The lad and the burning glass had grown to Archimedes.

What happened?

The plane neared the Mountain of Robold. The great bald summit and the four enormous globes of crystal. At least we so assume. We have Winter's word and that of the aviator that they were of the appearance of glass. Perhaps they were not; but we can assume it for description. So enormous that were they set upon a plain they would have overtopped the highest building ever constructed; though on the height of the mountain, and in its contrast, they were not much more than golf balls.

It was not their size but their effect that was startling. They were alive. At least that is what we have from Winters. Living, luminous, burning, twisting within with a thousand blending, iridescent beautiful colors. Not like electricity but something infinitely more powerful. Great mysterious magnets that Huyck had charged out of chaos. Glowing with the softest light; the whole mountain brightened as in a dream, and the town of Robold at its base lit up with a beauty that was past beholding.

It was new to Winters. The great buildings and the enormous machinery. Engines of strangest pattern, driven by forces that the rest of the world had not thought of. Not a sound; the whole works a complicated mass covering a hundred acres, driving with a silence that was magic. Not a whir nor friction. Like a living composite body pulsing and breathing the strange and mysterious force that had been evolved from Huyck's theory of kinetics. The four great steel conduits running from the globes down the side of the mountain. In the center, at a point midway between the globes, a massive steel needle hung on a pivot and pointed directly at the sun.

Winters and the aviator noted it and wondered. From the lower end of the needle was pouring a luminous stream of pale-blue opalescence, a stream much like a liquid, and of an unholy radiance. But it was not a liquid, nor fire, nor anything seen by man before.

It was force. We have no better description than the apt phrase of Winters. Charley Huyck was milking the sun, as it dropped from the end of the four living streams to the four globes that took it into storage. The four great, wonderful living globes; the four batteries; the very sight of their imprisoned beauty and power was magnetic.

The genius of Huyck and Robold! Nobody but the wildest dreamers would have conceived it. The life of the sun. And captive to man; at his will and volition. And in the next few minutes we were to lose it all! But in losing it we were to save ourselves. It was fate and nothing else.

There was but one thing more upon the mountain—the observatory and another needle apparently idle; but with a point much like a gigantic phonograph needle. It rose square out of the observatory, and to Winters it gave an impression of a strange gun, or some implement for sighting.

That was all. Coming with the speed that they were making, the airmen had no time for further investigation. But even this is comprehensive. Minus the force. If we only knew more about that or even its theory we might perhaps reconstruct the work of Charley Huyck and Dr. Robold.

They made the landing. Winters, with his nature, would be in at the finish; but Charley would not have it.

"It is death, Bob," he said. "You have a wife and babies. Go back to the world. Go back with all the speed you can get out of your motors. Get as far away as you can before the end comes."

With that he bade them a sad farewell. It was the last spoken word that the outside world had from Charley Huyck.

The last seen of him he was running up the steps of his office. As they soared away and looked back they could see men, the employees, scurrying about in frantic haste to their respective posts and stations. What was it all about? Little did the two aviators know. Little did they dream that it was the deciding stroke.

# 9

# THE MOST TERRIFIC MOMENT IN HISTORY

Still the great ball of Opalescence brooding over the Sargasso. Europe now was frozen, and though it was midsummer had gone into winter quarters. The Straits of Dover were no more. The waters had receded and one could walk, if careful, dryshod from the shores of France to the chalk cliffs of England. The Straits of Gibraltar had dried up. The Mediterranean completely land-locked, was cut off forever from the tides of the mother ocean.

The whole world going dry; not in ethics, but in reality. The great Vampire, luminous, beautiful beyond all ken and thinking, drinking up our lifeblood. The Atlantic a vast whirlpool.

A strange frenzy had fallen over mankind: men fought in the streets and died in madness. It was fear of the Great Unknown, and hysteria. At such a moment the veil of civilization was torn to tatters. Man was reverting to the primeval.

Then came the word from Charley Huyck; flashing and

repeating to every clime and nation. In its assurance it was almost as miraculous as the Vampire itself. For man had surrendered.

To the People of the World:

The strange and terrible Opalescence which, for the past seventy hours, has been playing havoc with the world, is not miracle, nor of the supernatural, but a mere manifestation and result of the application of celestial kinetics. Such a thing always was and always will be possible where there is intelligence to control and harness the forces that lie about us. Space is not space exactly, but an infinite cistern of unknown laws and forces. We may control certain laws on earth, but until we reach out farther we are but playthings.

Man is the intelligence of the earth. The time will come when he must be the intelligence of a great deal of space as well. At the present time you are merely fortunate and a victim of a kind fate. That I am the instrument of the earth's salvation is merely chance. The real man is Dr. Robold. When he picked me up on the streets I had no idea that the sequence of time would drift to this moment. He took me into his work and taught me.

Because he was sensitive and was laughed at, we worked in secret. And since his death, and out of respect to his memory, I have continued in the same manner. But I have written down everything, all the laws, computations, formulas—everything; and I am now willing it to mankind.

Robold had a theory on kinetics. It was strange at first and a thing to laugh at; but he reduced it to laws as potent and as inexorable as the laws of gravitation.

The luminous Opalescence that has almost destroyed us is but one of its minor manifestations. It is a message of sinister intelligence; for back of it all is an Intelligence. Yet it is not all sinister. It is self-preservation. The time is coming when eons of ages from now our own man will be forced to employ just such a weapon for his own preservation. Either that or we shall die of thirst and agony.

Let me ask you to remember now, that whatever you have suffered, you have saved a world. I shall now save you and the earth.

In the vaults you will find everything. All the knowledge and discoveries of the great Dr. Robold, plus a few minor findings by myself.

And now I bid you farewell. You shall soon be free.

CHARLEY HUYCK.

A strange message. Spoken over the wireless and flashed to every clime, it roused and revived the hope of mankind. Who was this Charley Huyck? Uncounted millions of men had never heard his name; there were but few, very few who had.

A message out of nowhere and of very dubious and doubtful explanation. Celestial kinetics! Undoubtedly. But the words explained nothing. However, man was ready to accept anything, so long as it saved him.

For a more lucid explanation we must go back to the Arizona observatory and Professor Ed. Williams. And a strange one it was truly; a certain proof that consciousness is more potent, far more so than mere material; also that many laws of our astronomers are very apt to be overturned in spite of their mathematics.

Charley Huyck was right. You cannot measure intelligence

with a yard-stick. Mathematics do not lie; but when applied to consciousness they are very likely to kick backward. That is precisely what had happened.

The suddenness of Huyck's departure had puzzled Professor Williams; that, and the note which he found upon the table. It was not like Charley to go off so in the stress of a moment. He had not even taken the time to get his hat and coat. Surely something was amiss.

He read the note carefully, and with a deal of wonder.

"Look these up. Keep by the lens. If the world goes up you will know I have not reached the mountain."

What did he mean? Besides, there was no data for him to work on. He did not know that an errant breeze had plumped the information behind the bookcase. Nevertheless he went into the observatory, and for the balance of the night stuck by the lens.

Now there are uncounted millions of stars in the sky. Williams had nothing to go by. A needle in the hay-stack were an easy task compared with the one that he was allotted. The flaming mystery, whatever it was that Huyck had seen, was not caught by the professor. Still, he wondered. "If the world goes up you will know I have not reached the mountain." What was the meaning?

But he was not worried. The professor loved Huyck as a visionary and smiled not a little at his delightful fancies. Doubtless this was one of them. It was not until the news came flashing out of Oakland that he began to take it seriously. Then followed the disappearance of Mount Heckla. "If the world goes up"—it began to look as if the words had meaning.

There was a frantic professor during the next few days. When he was not with the lens he was flashing out messages to the world for Charley Huyck. He did not know that Huyck was lying unconscious and almost dead upon the desert. That the world was coming to catastrophe he knew full well; but where was the man to save it? And most of all, what had his friend meant by the words, "look these up"?

Surely there must be some further information. Through the long, long hours he stayed with the lens and waited. And he found nothing.

It was three days. Who will ever forget them? Surely not Professor Williams. He was sweating blood. The whole world was going to pieces without the trace of an explanation. All the mathematics, all the accumulations of the ages had availed for nothing. Charley Huyck held the secret. It was in the stars, and not an astronomer could find it.

But with the seventeenth hour came the turn of fortune. The professor was passing through the office. The door was open, and the same fitful wind which had played the original prank was now just as fitfully performing restitution. Williams noticed a piece of paper protruding from the back of the bookcase and fluttering in the breeze. He picked it up. The first words that he saw were in the handwriting of Charley Huyck. He read:

"In the last extremity—in the last phase when there is no longer any water on the earth; when even the oxygen of the atmospheric envelope has been reduced to a minimum—man, or whatever form of intelligence is then upon the earth, must go back to the laws which governed his forebears. Necessity must ever be the law of evolution. There will be no water upon the earth, but there will be an unlimited quantity elsewhere.

"By that time, for instance, the great planet, Jupiter, will be in just a convenient state for exploitation. Gaseous now, it will be, by that time, in just about the stage when the steam and water are condensing into ocean. Eons of millions of years away in the days of dire necessity. By that time the intelligence and consciousness of the earth will have grown equal to the task.

"It is a thing to laugh at (perhaps) just at present. But when we consider the ratio of man's advance in the last hundred years, what will it be in a billion? Not all the laws of the universe have been discovered, by any means. At present we know nothing. Who can tell?

"Aye, who can tell? Perhaps we ourselves have in store the fate we would mete out to another. We have a very dangerous neighbor close beside us. Mars is in dire straits for water. And we know there is life on Mars and intelligence! The very fact on its face proclaims it. The oceans have dried up; the only way they have of holding life is by bringing their water from the polar snow-caps. Their canals pronounce an advanced state of cooperative intelligence; there is life upon Mars and in an advanced stage of evolution.

"But how far advanced? It is a small planet, and consequently eons of ages in advance of the earth's evolution. In the nature of things Mars cooled off quickly, and life was possible there while the earth was yet a gaseous mass. She has gone to her maturity and into her retrogression; she is approaching her end. She has had less time to produce intelligence than intelligence will have—in the end—upon the earth.

"How far has this intelligence progressed? That is the question. Nature is a slow worker. It took eons of ages to put life upon the earth; it took eons of more ages to make this life conscious. How far will it go? How far has it gone on Mars?"

That was as far the the comments went. The professor dropped his eyes to the rest of the paper. It was a map of the face of Mars, and across its center was a black cross scratched by the dull point of a soft pencil.

He knew the face of Mars. It was the Ascraeus Lucus. The

oasis at the juncture of a series of canals running much like the spokes of a wheel. The great Uranian and Alander Canals coming in at about right angles.

In two jumps the professor was in the observatory with the great lens swung to focus. It was the great moment out of his lifetime, and the strangest and most eager moment, perhaps, ever lived by any astronomer. His fingers fairly twitched with tension. There before his view was the full face of our Martian neighbor!

But was it? He gasped out a breath of startled exclamation. Was it Mars that he gazed at; the whole face, the whole thing had been changed before him.

Mars has ever been red. Viewed through the telescope it has had the most beautiful tinge imaginable, red ochre, the weird tinge of the desert in sunset. The color of enchantment and of hell!

For it is so. We know that for ages and ages the planet has been burning up; that life was possible only in the dry sea-bottoms and under irrigation. The rest, where the continents once were, was blazing desert. The redness, the beauty, the enchantment that we so admired was burning hell.

All this had changed.

Instead of this was a beautiful shade of iridescent green. The red was gone forever. The great planet standing in the heavens had grown into infinite glory. Like the great Dog Star transplanted.

The professor sought out the Ascraeus Lucus. It was hard to find. The whole face had been transfigured; where had been canals was now the beautiful sheen of green and verdure. He realized what he was beholding and what he had never dreamed of seeing; the seas of Mars filled up.

With the stolen oceans our grim neighbor had come back to youth. But how had it been done. It was horror for our world. The great luminescent ball of Opalescence! Europe frozen and

New York a mass of ice. It was the earth's destruction. How long could the thing keep up; and whence did it come? What was it?

He sought for the Ascraeus Lucus. And he beheld a strange sight. At the very spot where should have been the juncture of the canals he caught what at first looked like a pin-point flame, a strange twinkling light with flitting glow of Opalescence. He watched it, and he wondered. It seemed to the professor to grow; and he noticed that the green about it was of different color. It was winking, like a great force, and much as if alive; baneful.

It was what Charley Huyck had seen. The professor thought of Charley. He had hurried to the mountain. What could Huyck, a mere man, do against a thing like this? There was naught to do but sit and watch it drink of our lifeblood. And then—

It was the message, the strange assurance that Huyck was flashing over the world. There was no lack of confidence in the words he was speaking. "Celestial Kinetics," so that was the answer! Certainly it must be so with the truth before him. Williams was a doubter no longer. And Charley Huyck could save them. The man he had humored. Eagerly he waited and stuck by the lens. The whole world waited.

It was perhaps the most terrific moment since creation. To describe it would be like describing doomsday. We all of us went through it, and we all of us thought the end had come; that the earth was torn to atoms and to chaos.

The State of Colorado was lurid with a red light of terror; for a thousand miles the flame shot above the earth and into space. If ever spirit went out in glory that spirit was Charley Huyck! He had come to the moment and to Archimedes. The whole world rocked to the recoil. Compared to it the mightiest earthquake was but a tender shiver. The consciousness of the earth had spoken!

The professor was knocked upon the floor. He knew not what had happened. Out of the windows and to the north the flame of Colorado, like the whole world going up. It was the last moment. But he was a scientist to the end. He had sprained his ankle and his face was bleeding; but for all that he struggled, fought his way to the telescope. And he saw:

The great planet with its sinister, baleful, wicked light in the center, and another light vastly larger covering up half of Mars. What was it? It was moving. The truth set him almost to shouting.

It was the answer of Charley Huyck and of the world. The light grew smaller, smaller, and almost to a pin-point on its way to Mars.

The real climax was in silence. And of all the world only Professor Williams beheld it. The two lights coalesced and spread out; what it was on Mars, of course, we do not know.

But in a few moments all was gone. Only the green of the Martian Sea winked in the sunlight. The luminous opal was gone from the Sargasso. The ocean lay in peace.

It was a terrible three days. Had it not been for the work of Robold and Huyck life would have been destroyed. The pity of it that all of their discoveries have gone with them. Not even Charley realized how terrific the force he was about to loosen.

He had carefully locked everything in vaults for a safe delivery to man. He had expected death, but not the cataclysm. The whole of Mount Robold was shorn away; in its place we have a lake fifty miles in diameter.

So much for celestial kinetics.

And we look to a green and beautiful Mars. We hold no enmity. It was but the law of self-preservation. Let us hope they have enough water; and that their seas will hold. We don't blame them, and we don't blame ourselves, either for that matter. We need what we have, and we hope to keep it.